MUMS DON'T FART, Okay!!

BONNEY
PRESS

Lisa Regan • Agnès Ernoult

For my mum...

E.M.

Published by Bonney Press
an imprint of Hinkler Pty Ltd
45–55 Fairchild Street
Heatherton Victoria 3202 Australia
www.hinkler.com

BONNEY
PRESS

Author: Lisa Regan
Illustrator: Agnès Ernoult
Editorial: Emily Murray

ISBN: 978 1 4889 0621 3

Printed and bound in China

Join Marty and his wizard friends; they are a cheeky bunch.
They're gathered in his bedroom, casting spells and having lunch.

'Remember when we proved girls fart?
It was just as we had guessed.

Fairy flumps and mermaid trumps –
the princess toot was best!'

'I've been thinking about that,' said Sam,
who swivelled in his seat.

'We followed girls and animals, but
our test was incomplete.

We didn't learn if adults fart!
More research should be done.

What if teachers let off gas?
What **about**...

your **MUM?!**'

The boys all gasped.
'Imagine that! Surely mums just don't!'

'Let's find Marty's mum and question her.'

'You can ask – I won't!'

No boy would volunteer, so Fizz signalled for a pause.

'There's only one thing for it. We'll decide by drawing straws.'

Ethan was the chosen one. He nervously stepped forward.

'Er, Mrs Jones, if you don't mind,
can I please have a word?

Girls and boys fart all the time –
it gives us great delight.
But we weren't sure if ladies trump, or if
they're too polite?'

Mrs Jones turned very red. She couldn't believe her ears.
'Of course they don't, you cheeky boys!

Now go and play, my dears.'

The boys retreated, unconvinced. Could Marty's mum be trusted?
She might be covering up the truth; she did seem very flustered.

Mrs Jones was clearing up and couldn't see the boys.

As she bent to move some papers, her bottom made a noise.

'**Granddad Bob, you're snoring!**'
She tried to pass the blame.

But the gang could smell the evidence, and didn't believe her claim.

Next, they searched for Fizz's mum,
and found her in the garden.

Fizz blurted,
'Do mums fart?'

Mum gasped,
'I beg your pardon?'

**'Sorry, Mum, but we're intrigued.
We just really want to know.'**

His mother shook her head at him and told them they should go.

The boys snuck off, out of sight, and crouched on bended knees.
They saw Mum's laundry on the line, blowing in the breeze.

Except, there was no wind today! So what did those sheets prove?
That his mum was telling fibs and her fartnado made them move?

Fizz's mum flew off to work. The gang must find out more.

They tailed her through the broom park and up to the main door.

As she hurried through the spinning door they saw it turning faster.
Mrs Wright had made it whirl by letting off a blaster!

Mum took a seat behind her desk, as the boys came through the door.

prrp

They grinned as Mum let out a toot and zoomed across the floor.

Stifling laughs, the boys stayed still as Mum reached for her phone.
Prrp prrp! they heard. They chuckled more.
'That's a new ringtone!'

prrp prrp

The boys then went to find Sam's mum. She was with his little brother. Sam claimed that she never fluffed. 'No way - not <u>my</u> mother!'

But as the concert reached the end with the trumpet's final hoot,
Someone in the audience let out a mighty *toot*.

It was Sam's face that turned bright red.
'I can't believe she did it!

It must be mum that makes home smell,
and all this time she hid it!

We tend to blame our dog a lot
for being such a stinker,

but now I wonder who is worse –
my mother or poor Tinker?'

Ethan's mum was with her friends. They ordered drinks and cake.

'Is that my Mum who's made a smell?
Oh, for goodness sake!'

The group stood up to say goodbye. They gathered for a selfie.
'Someone's guffed! What a stink!
More like hashtag SMELLfie!'

Then all the boy's mums gathered for their weekly yoga class.
The boys raced off to take a look, their noses against the glass.

The row of ladies bent and stretched for their 'salute the sun'.
But yoga made them all relax: mass trumpeting had begun!

'We've proved our point. You mums _do_ toot.
Of that, there is no doubt.

You cannot hide your farts, for like the truth,
they _will_ come out!'